REAL FISHERMEN
ARE NEVER THIN

by
John Davis

Best Wishes
Sincerely
John Davis

PINEGROVE
PUBLISHING

PO Box 557 • Winona Lake, IN 46590

To
Dr. E. William Male
Fisherman, Scholar, Friend

First printing — Feb., 1993
Second Printing — Oct., 1993

Published by   Pinegrove Publishing
                P.O. Box 557
                Winona Lake, IN 46590 USA

ISBN 0-9635865-0-5

TABLE OF CONTENTS

The Ol' Scribe at Work

Introduction

I love the outdoors.

In fact, I probably would have been committed to Harry's Happy Farm a long time ago were it not for my therapeutic passion for nature.

This book is a collection of various lighthearted glimpses at the world of the outdoors which have appeared in my weekly Warsaw *Times-Union* column, "Outdoor Scene" during the past 12 years.

The city of Warsaw is nestled among 105 natural lakes in Kosciusko County, Indiana, and is a fisherman's paradise. Steeped in rich tradition, this city of 17,000 is friendly, progressive and culturally diverse.

Nowhere is that diversity more evident than at one of its most famous food emporiums, Breadings' Cigar Store, located in an old building on Center Street. It has been there for ages and attracts men of all walks of life for both food and games of dominoes. Some anthropologists claim there are missing links in the geological record, but I have seen most of those links walking around in Breadings'.

The mysterious charm of this place has attracted reporters and journalists from all over the state and even brought Douglas Kiker of NBC television there for a special program.

It's where fishermen gather to exchange lies, lawyers to develop strategy, politicians to learn what's really going on and farmers to wait for their crops to grow. In the following pages you will see frequent references to the store and its co-owners, Burleigh Burgh and Craig Smith.

Our town is full of characters and celebrities which are, at times, hard to distinguish. Some of their names will appear as well. For the most part, however, my cast of fictitious characters like Harvy Moot, Melvin Mossback, Hiram Hackwood and Dork Featherstone will be on center stage. It's safer that way.

There are also several references to Arab friendships I have developed during service as a senior staff member on nine archaeological expeditions to the Middle East. Such memories, both lighthearted and sad, will help broaden our appreciation of American outdoor life.

I wish to give special thanks to the staff, students and faculty at Grace College and Grace Theological Seminary in Winona Lake, Indiana, who have been a great encouragement over the years. Gratitude is also expressed to Professor Frank Benyousky and Mr. Joel Curry for reading the manuscript and making valuable suggestions. I am also most grateful to Kevin Carter for the preparation of the cover and superb illustrations and to Brenda Minard for quality typesetting and page design.

Finally, many thanks to my friend, Eldon Kibbey, for valuable suggestions and corrections for the second printing.

My greatest wish, however, is that the reading of this volume will bring a smile to your face, brighten your day and develop a new passion for the great outdoors.

If all this occurs, my reward for writing this book will be complete.

The Well-Rounded Angler

Real Fishermen
are Never Thin

Joggers, tennis players, skiers, and fashion models are thin, but that is because they don't eat real food.

They nibble ever so daintily on alfalfa sprouts and consume tiny portions of yogurt or cottage cheese.

Only crusty ol' fishermen eat real food and as a result are never thin.

Real food is always cooked in generous portions of lard over a campfire and will regularly have a green worm or caterpillar floating motionless on the top.

Alfalfa sprouts, parsley, cabbage and celery can never be considered real food because they do not brown well in lard and rarely combine effectively with sauteed caterpillars or bugs.

Joggers, racquetball players and hair stylists are thin and generally undernourished because they don't eat enough calories.

Real fishermen, on the other hand, make it a point to eat generous portions of pork, moose, 'possum, carp and deer cooked in deep lard. The side dish is always fried potatoes with bacon and onions seasoned with heaping spoonfuls of salt, pepper and other spices found in the cabin or tackle box. That is why fishermen are not thin.

Food columnist, Marcia Adams, that delightful lady of delectable dishes, provides readers with some of the best culinary offerings in the mid west. I just don't have the heart to tell her that thousands of real fishermen are passing up her recipes due to the absence of substantial quantities of salt, pepper and lard.

The physical demands on the fisherman require that he have a substantial intake of quality calories every day. Petite wives, of course, do not fully understand this important principle and regularly hound Mr. Outdoors to trim down. Little do they know they are putting a real fisherman's piscatorial talent at risk with such reckless suggestions.

My friend, Hiram Hackwood, is a good example of this situation. His wife, Rosebud, is so skinny that when she wears a fur coat she looks like a pipe cleaner.

The Hackwood kitchen, I should note, is not your average food processing station. Rosebud owns no stove or oven, but has equipped herself with a microwave unit, stoneware crockery, a minitoaster, four blenders, two vegetable choppers and a five-gallon yogurt cooler.

Every can or box on the shelves reads in bright red, "low-cholesterol," "high-fiber," "low-fat," or "vitamin-enriched."

This moving piece of poetry appears on the wall

above their solid oak table:
>Mary had a little watch
>She swallowed it one day
>Now she's taking Epsom salts
>To pass the time away.

Rosebud was recently heard grumbling, "Hiram, you're so fat you're beginning to look like an overweight walrus out of water. Why don't you trim down with this wonderful popcorn and grapefruit diet? Your lumpy anatomy is an embarrassment to my mother."

"The problem is not with my weight, but with gravity," he responded authoritatively. "The local field of gravity to too great for my body mass and it is distorting my true physique. As soon as I can finagle a way to reduce the force of gravity in our area, I will look like Mr. Muscle, 1988."

Rosebud did not say a word. The power of Hiram's scientific argument must have precluded further debate on the issue.

Coffee is another vital component of a fishermen's diet. You will find bass boats without coolers, depth finders, oarlocks and live wells, but never without a coffee-stained mug.

Real fishermen drink gallons of black coffee to maintain the necessary stamina for long hours of casting and conversation. Coffee stimulates the appetite which leads to sandwich-munching and cracker-crunching until the next pan full of lard fried catfish can be inhaled on shore.

There are, of course, good reasons why real fishermen shun a svelte silhouette. The thin rod man would be a high risk passenger in a bass boat on a windy day. Maintaining vertical stability could prove impossible and every cast might pose a threat to the safety of others in the boat.

The idea that real fishermen do not burn up calories during a normal fishing day is nasty rumor which I have traced back to a small minority of lawyers and bankers who eat at the rear table of Breadings' Cigar Store.

My meticulous calculations indicate that, prior to, and during his fishing expedition, the average angler takes in 7,089 calories from consuming shore lunches, mass quantities of hamburgers fried in lard, sweet rolls, cans of pop, candy bars and potato chips.

Assuming that the same angler loads and unloads his own boat, has a hand starting motor, casts crank baits for at least six hours, lifts the anchor nine times, drives to and from the boat launch, pulls in ten bass weighing an average of two pounds each, and cleans five bass and 62 bluegills, he would have burnt up a total of 7,089 calories!

The net calorie gain from his fishing trip, therefore, would be zero.

So you wives, take it easy on Mr. Outdoors. What you regard as unnecessary flab is actually body mass strategically organized to provide maximum stability in a bass boat.

Anatomical bulges are not the by-product of culinary indulgence, but the uncontrollable effect of gravitational force.

Real fishermen are never thin.

Skinny anglers are deeply suspect.

A Breadings' Blue Plate Special

Fine Dining

I must tell you, I'm not crazy about heartburn, and I find it particularly distressing when I've paid $21.95 for a meal at some over-decorated food emporium and then have to grab the Rolaids before I even pay the bill.

The agony is particularly acute when the food is dull and the conversation boring.

Frankly, gang, I'm weary of perfect toast, eggs with useless orange wedges and sprigs of dried parsley draped over half my food.

Lively and engaging conversation with people who sparkle with imagination can take your mind off boring food, but if you end up with a bunch of cultural clunkers, you're in deep trouble because you then begin thinking about the taste of what you've been chewing on for the past five minutes.

Even decor plays a role in the success or failure of an evening's repast. Some restaurants, with their plush carpets and elegant chandeliers, are about as

11

exciting as Lenin's tomb. What chance does food
have in that sort of environment?

I've been known to remedy all this, however,
with an occasional swing into that unmarked male
bastion of philosophical dialogue and outlandish
humor—Breadings' Cigar Store.

Snobs and other cultural obscurantists will lift
their powdered noses into air at such a suggestion,
but the ol' scribe knows whereof he speaks.

I am always amazed at all the people who will
drive to Fort Wayne, South Bend or even Chicago for
a classy meal, then spend the entire next day brag-
ging about the superb $27.95 "blackened fish" or
"blackened chicken" they had the night before.

And you think these folks really have a grip on
culinary creativity?

Look, for the price of a small paperback book, I
can have all my food blackened at Breadings' and
served on coffee stained-tables that cry out with
tradition.

Not only is blackened food one of the notable
features of this dining spot, but Breadings' always
blackens and thickens the coffee as well.

I don't want to overstate the case, but Hiram
Hackwood recently drank only one cup of that brew
and stayed awake during an entire Ross Perot speech!

There is a air of mystery that surrounds a meal in
this anthropological museum of misfits. Guru of
Grease and Master Chef, Burleigh Burgh, contends
that his secret recipes cannot be found anywhere else
in the universe.

His menu specials include, "Outdoor Surprise,"
"Woodland Wonders" and "Meaty Magic." I have
always wondered about the exotic tastes that bubble
forth from these dishes. I suspected that something

was amiss when all the ants in the place began bringing their own lunches.

It was not until I was recently able to sneak down into the basement and do some big-time investigation that my curiosity was satisfied.

There was a lot of copper tubing, several large metal drums and about 50 bags of mash in one corner. I concluded Burleigh must be into raising chickens on the side.

On one of the shelves, however, I saw a stack of road-kill possums—very thin and very crispy. The Armstrong Tire marks were still visible on several of the bodies, and someone had labeled them, "Wildlife Wonders."

Then, I spotted large supplies of cans marked "Unadulterated Road Kill," and knew immediately what had been floating around in my "Outdoor Surprise Soup."

You might think these startling discoveries sent the ol' scribe into gastronomic despair and disappointment.

Not at all.

I just realized that I had been dining in the presence of a brilliant chef and business entrepreneur. Burleigh can price exotic dishes at one-third the Chicago rate and still turn a cool 60 percent profit.

The *tour de force* of this unique eating establishment, however, has to be cultural sophistication and intellectual ambiance.

In most of Warsaw's dining establishments, bankers whine about interest rates, real estate types groan over declining prices and everybody gripes about taxes.

In dramatic contrast to such shallow fare, Breadings' intellectuals can usually be found hotly debating life's deeper issues. Just last week the local sophists were asking whether the swing on a tree rises higher when the tree grows. Many hairs were split over that one.

There are no menus, written bills or waitresses at this emporium which has captured the attention of newspapers and magazines in the area, to say nothing of NBC television.

Alka-Seltzer scalpers are always outside and are known to make hundreds of dollars a day.

The one touch of sanity and efficiency in the place is provided by co-owner, Craig Smith, who does ten jobs while Burleigh carries on verbal battle with three customers at once.

Ladies rarely wander into Breadings', but when they do, it is fair to say they take meaningful memories home with them. One husband wanted to take his wife in there for a birthday lunch, but with a gasp she responded, "they chew tobacco in that place!"

I guess that's true, alright, but there are always a lot of good seats on the dry side of the spittoons.

Restaurants with squeaky clean floors make me uneasy. No problem here. The floor is always littered with napkins, cigarette butts, newspapers and other assorted debris adding real charm to the place.

An innocent salesman wandered in one day and asked "Where is the ash tray?"

"You're standing in it," was Burleigh's reply.

Of course, the real reason I dine at this most exotic of Warsaw's restaurants is because of the goofy and rare outdoor types who frequent the store and provide an endless stream of information for this writer.

Some folks' idea of a rich gourmet experience is noshing fettucini at an overpriced dive in Chicago.

In the humble opinion of this writer, however, Warsaw's Breadings' Cigar Store wins the fine dining award hands down.

World's Greatest Vegetable

Asparagus

I love asparagus.

This plant, which has driven taste buds into frenzied delight ever since the Romans began serving it 2000 years ago, is majestic in appearance and succulent in taste.

The domestication of this elegant vegetable is usually attributed to the Greeks, who also employed it for medicinal purposes.

Let's face it. An asparagus casserole featuring delicately trimmed stems dripping with cheddar cheese is the envy of the civilized world.

Already, however, I can sense outrage on the part of potato lovers everywhere at the mere mention of asparagus superiority, but one must face basic botanical and culinary facts.

Just consider the stately stalk's nutritional features. It is low in calories but contains large amounts of calcium and phosphorus, to say nothing of generous supplies of vitamins A, C and B (niacin).

Almost any soil can be used to raise this plant, which grows from six inches to two feet tall and produces edible stems for more than 15 years before an appropriate burial is required.

So intense is the affection of Hoosiers and Michiganders for this vibrant vegetable that they will brave early June rains in wet fields just to collect a handful of wild asparagus for their table.

At unearthly early morning hours they gaze across the fields with bloodshot eyes in search of the telltale signs of an asparagus bed. Last year's crop will conveniently leave stalks with a golden tint and tumbleweed appearance which, when spotted, will signal a charge into the grass with pan and scissors in hand.

The relentless search by this soggy army for the well-hidden tender green stems frequently evokes questions from mystified observers like, "Why in the world are you cutting that asparagus in a heavy rain at 5:00 a.m.?"

"Because it's there," a little old lady will scream back triumphantly shaking a handful of freshly cut sprouts at the noisy intruders.

"Are Hoosiers loosing their sanity?" a friend of mine wanted to know as he watched two elderly men happily snipping asparagus along railroad tracks near Warsaw.

"No, these highly intelligent, culinary-minded craftsman are harvesting the world's most magnificent vegetable," I answered with a knowing and appropriate dignity.

He gave me the strangest look and then decided to move to topics less encumbered with controversy, like politics, women's liberation, Pentagon efficiency, and Rush Limbaugh.

Shallow-minded critics of the asparagus' superiority in the vegetable kingdom will inevitably point to the noticeable impact it has on urine. (In our fearless commitment to complete investigation, we outdoor writers are obligated to mention such things).

That pungent odor, which has caused some to begin thinking of their yearly checkup, is actually produced by what chemists call methylmercaptan-saturated liquids.

I recently learned, however, that methylmercaptan-influenced urine is not universally acknowledged, even by sportsmen who are in sparkling health.

With nagging curiosity, I began to do some research while lecturing in London this past summer, and to my utter amazement, I discovered a feature article in the *British Medical Journal* entitled, "A Polymorphism of the Ability to Smell Urinary Metabolites of Asparagus."

It seems that this chemical anomaly did not escape the watchful eye of the English medical community, which, with the help of 328 sniffing volunteers, proceeded to untangle this nose-oriented paradox.

The considered conclusion was that, indeed, some people can devour a whole bushel of asparagus and never be offended by its odorous aftereffects. Their peculiar good fortune, however, has not occurred because they failed to produce a significant quantity of methylmercaptan; they simply were incapable of smelling it!

At this point, I suspect that segments of the Warsaw population blessed with such olfactory immunity will be wondering what in the world I've been talking about.

Now we come to the crux of this whole matter. Since the asparagus is blessed with such aesthetic beauty, mouth-watering delectability and memorable aftereffects, it seems high time that it be declared the official vegetable of the city of Warsaw.

We have state flowers and birds, but here is our Mayor's grand opportunity to blaze a new cultural trail by naming the stately asparagus as the symbol of Warsaw's greatness. This is a plant with undeniable durability and universal appeal. If he would make such a declaration, city governments throughout the state would be overcome with jealousy and attempt to duplicate his far-sighted decision.

But it would be too late.

Other cities could only own the lesser veggies—onions might work for South Bend, eggplant for Fort Wayne and cabbage for Indianapolis.

Forget the sewer projects, city parks, and shopping malls, Mr. Mayor, and with an eye toward really significant priorities, name the asparagus the official city vegetable. Every dedicated Republican will sing your praises and elephants the world over will face Warsaw and salute.

Asparagus and Warsaw were made for each other.

Bass Are Basically Dumb

Indiana's Smartest Fish

All we hear these days is "bass this and bass that."

It seems that anglers are making an undue fuss over a fish that has as its most distinguishing feature a big mouth.

Tournaments are held for this fish, clubs have been formed in its honor, millions of dollars are spent each year on lures to catch it and even the Indiana Department of Natural Resources has become a partner in this hysteria.

Respected DNR fishery biologists are guilty of complicity in this angling conspiracy when they do research on this critter, publish detailed studies on its habits and habitat, and engage in a lot of brouhaha regarding size limits.

All the time, the handsome carp, a sleek, durable, dynamo of the deep, is totally ignored.

It just isn't fair.

I realize this is a morally complex issue, but it is

high time proper attention be given to this golden example of piscatorial power.

Fishing magazines are saturated with bass anglers gurgling such profound phrases as, "that's a purty fish, good buddy," or "you'ns really got a fat hawg there." Then, too, there are the multitude of articles just dripping with such intricate topics as "Hawgs are Pigs on Pork."

The verbal artistry of the modern bass angler is only surpassed by the mumbo-jumbo of the fishery biologist who utters expressions of ecstasy when he collects five bass in 30 minutes of electroshocking.

Biologist, Ed Braun, is especially guilty of this; I know from having been with him on various lakes during fish population studies. When a four pound bass is taken, he gurgles like a baby with a new rubber ducky, but let me haul up a gorgeous 15-pound carp and all you get is a groan.

The result of years of prejudicial thinking on this matter makes it very difficult for the total angler to pursue the carp without receiving a permanent blot on his character.

I know I will incur the wrath of some portion of the 27 million bass groupies, many of whom willingly spend up to $30,000 on a boat, rods and lures to catch a 12-inch monster. But the glory of the carp will never be known if someone does not step forward at great risk to body and soul to take up its cause.

Do you have any idea why so many people fish for the largemouth bass? The reason is simple, it's easy to catch. Do you know why it's easy to catch? It's dumb.

There, I said it. Bass are dumb.

The proof for this eminently perceptive assertion is overwhelming. Bass will bite plastic, wood, metal and cloth in all kinds of nutty shapes. So stupid is this specie that DNR biologists have to set size limits on it, otherwise this ichthyonic ignoramus would be wiped out in one season.

Do you see carp running after metal spinner baits or plastic plugs? When was the last time you saw a carp smash a lure designed to look like a mouse?

It will not happen because carp are too smart! Their brilliant sense of discernment prevents them from falling prey to depth finders, pH meters, temperature gauges, plastic worms, metal jigs and buzz baits. They don't need size limits or biologists to protect them.

The good ol' carp can live for 20 years or more in muddy lakes with mucky bottoms and still swim around with a smile on its face. Largemouth bass, on the other hand, make a big fuss about clean water, adequate vegetation, quality forage and durable structure. Bass are promoted as highly intelligent creatures, but I regard that notion as nothing more than a myth created by unsuccessful anglers.

So what does the lofty carp get for his efforts at reproduction and survival in the worst of lakes? Eradication, that's what.

Take, for example, the carnage inflicted on carp by the DNR Rotenone application at two local lakes several years ago. Dead golden bodies floated to the surface by the thousands after having outsmarted bass and bluegill fishermen, survived bitter winters and endured contaminated sludge. Biologists and regular people stood on the banks and cheered.

I walked along those soggy banks with a Zebco hat over my heart and grieved as this noble creature was scooped up and put in garbage cans. Oh, the agony of it all!

Just consider, for a moment, the virtues of the carp. It is prolific, intelligent, easy to recognize, edible and a good fighter.

Why, then, didn't the DNR ever include this magnificent creature in one of its "Fish of the Week" selections?

My eyes lit up and my heart pounded with expectation, however, when I received the 1987 and 1989 DNR reports on Triploid Grass Carp. That momentary ecstasy was dashed to smithereens when I realized the agency was only interested in their bodies and how much vegetation they could eat in a natural lake.

Maybe, just maybe, this summer some angler will hook onto a giant carp and realize that life is more than bass and Bill Dance lures.

But then again, who am I to argue this issue on intellectual grounds? I still have 500 shares of Edsel stock and a partnership in a bait and boat shop on the Dead Sea, and I was the one who predicted a second term for president George Bush.

The Hat: An Angler's Best Friend

Why Fishermen
Wear Hats

A fisherman might forget his lunch, wife, map, or medicine on his way to Winona Lake for an outing, but never his hat.

Fishing hats are generally very old, bent and dirty, and they all emit odors only an angler could love or identify.

Sociologists have yet to explain why the American male can let cars, radios, vacuum cleaners, houses and jewels come and go, but devotedly hangs onto his lumpy, tattered fishing hat forever.

My wife insists that anglers are basically insecure and the hat serves as sort of a mental security blanket. "Fishermen hate rejection," she explained recently. "They know they're going to be ignored by even moderately intelligent bluegills, and just the thought of rejection by a woman causes them to break out in a cold sweat. A fishing hat, however, has never rejected anyone."

"Fishermen wouldn't think of being seen in public sucking their thumbs and cuddling their fishing towels, so they all wear fishing hats to calm their anxieties and give them a sense of identity," she concludes.

My wife claims that she reached that conclusion from personal observation — a notion which I am compelled to vigorously deny.

Young, innocent types naively assume that fishing hats are worn to keep the sun out of one's eyes. "Yep, a good hat will improve your fishing 40-50 percent," Hiram Hackwood used to tell me. "You can see into the water to locate fish better, but most important, it prevents headaches that rob you of the ability to really concentrate."

Before you begin cheering Hackwood's logic, I should point out that his wife, Gardenia, who never wears a hat while fishing, out-catches him on every outing.

Then, there are those who wear hats because the pros do. Just let Bill Dance catch an eight-pound largemouth on his Saturday TV program while wearing a hat with a "T" on it, and I'll guarantee you that 80 percent of the bass fishermen on Lake Wawasee will have the same kind of hat on the following day.

My friend, Tyrone Typo, says his hat keeps his hair from blowing into his eyes while fishing. But the roof on Tyrone's mental living room is only covered around the edges so his perspective on this issue seems rather suspect.

Then, there are those who wear fishing hats for fashion reasons only. My wife fits into this category.

"No, I don't want the brown hat, it clashes with my jacket and eyes," she announced as we prepared to go to Center Lake. "I want the red one because I'm a 'winter person' and it goes with my dark hair."

The fact that bluegills are not fashion conscious, or the fact that most of her dark hair will not be visible while wearing a hat, seem not to bother her, and I'm certainly not going to press the issue. We outdoor writers may not be mental giants, but we're not stupid either!

Of course, there will always be some fly-fishing purists who will stare straight into your eyes with a disgustingly serious look and claim you need to wear a hat so you have a place on which to hang your flies.

They are already cluttered up with 37 little cans hanging from their vests and 53 plastic boxes stuffed into their pockets, and they expect us to swallow that hat theory?!

Frustrated by unproductive research into this sociologically complex issue, I decided to visit Warsaw's famous "think-tank"— Breadings' Cigar Store. Here, indeed, I would have access to some of the area's most brilliant minds; surely, they could illuminate this murky topic. Boy, did they!

It seems that fishing hats are perceived to have a lot to do with the issue of baldness or, I should say, the concealment thereof.

"Most fishermen are either bald or well on their way to having their lawns disappear," Burleigh Burgh, Breadings' overrated five-star chef, argued while waving a slice of burnt toast in the air. "The wind can be cold or the sun very hot out on the water, and those boys have to protect their tender tops."

On the surface, it would seem that there is a bit of logic in this observation by Warsaw's guru of grease, but the rest of the Breadings' brain trust differs strongly on the issue. It seems that Burgh's culinary clientele fall into two philosophical camps on this cranial conundrum.

One group argues that fishing hats prevent baldness, while the other maintains that they cause it. So, which is it?

Subsequent to Burgh's toast-waving assertion, this most compelling of contemporary questions became the subject of a rather long and vigorous debate among the philosophical wits assembled at Breadings'.

Tommy Tunk, whose thatch is so thin only a loving mother could spot the remaining sprigs, argued, "I wouldn't have an eight-inch part in my hair today if I had worn a hat while fishing. The sun baked my scalp and the wind blew away the roasted hairs."

"The sun didn't bake your scalp, you ol' coot, it shish-kebabed your brain," his fishing partner, Mike Mildew, fired back. "You've always worn a hat and that's why you have a nude noggin' today."

"It's a scientific fact that tight hats reduce circulation to the scalp, and that causes loss of lawn," he concluded.

About that time, Harvy Moot, senior editor of the *Fogbottom Gazette* came stumbling in and deposited his lumpy body on a chair at the back table.

"Hey Harvy, you're a college graduate, what do you think of Mike Mildew's theory," Hiram Hackwood wanted to know.

"Duhhhhh, dat idee has got somethin' to it, but you never can be sure," he responded with scientific precision and notable philosophical profundity.

Returning to the debate was Warsaw's answer to Julia Child and holder of the 1992 Stomach Pump Award, Burleigh Burgh. "Yeah, I remember reading about that scalpo-pathological syndrome in the *Jour-*

nal of the American Medical Association. It said that reduction of circulation leads to deprivation of corpuscle supply resulting in alopecia."

For all those who don't own dictionaries, alopecia is an eight-cylinder word that refers to loss of hair.

Now, friends, before you reach the ridiculous conclusion that Burgh is some sort of medical Einstein, you should know that on a recent I.Q. test administered by Dr. Marvin Mildew, he registered three points above a can of Spam.

The statistical accuracy of that test was verified by the recent revelation that Burgh thought, "Roe vs. Wade" were the options that George Washington had when he was about to cross the Delaware River.

Fishermen, who become aware that their hairline is in full retreat, often attempt to master the situation with humor. "They don't put marble tops on cheap furniture," or "grass doesn't grow on busy streets," will be their retort while combing their scalp with a wash cloth. What is never acknowledged is that grass doesn't grow on dead ends, either.

Dork Featherstone suspects that the tight-hat/loss-of-circulation theory is nothing more than subversive propaganda circulated by the nose drop industry to entice men to quit wearing hats.

"Once a poor slob shelves his fishing hat, it isn't long before he develops sinus trouble or a perpetual cold," he explains.

Breadings' maitre d' and celebrated coffee splasher, Craig Smith, suggests that "when you wear a fishing hat, the hair follicles all go to sleep in the darkness and no longer produce hair. You need to stimulate the scalp to reawaken them and keep your hair coming."

Resident bluegill whiz, Harvy Moot, actually

bought that crock of baloney and invested $199 in a
two-month supply of "Helsinki Formula 1227C,"
which his wife dutifully rubbed on every morning.

When Harvy entered Breadings' last Wednes-
day, what remaining hair he had looked like it had
been arranged with a trowel. Worse yet, he reeked
with odors so pungent that they caused the paint to
peal on the west wall of the Burgh's food emporium.
The cream was noticeable even if the hair was not!

Frankly, the Arab explanation of baldness is as
credible as any I've encountered. My friend,
Mohammed Yasin of Amman, Jordan, used to claim
that when fishermen reach 50, their hair grows in
rather than out. If they have gray matter (brains and
wisdom), their hair turns gray. If there is nothing
there, the hair disappears!

It was apparent that the wise men resident at
Breadings' were not moving toward a meaningful
conclusion to the fishing hat issue, so I decided to
seek out a feminine touch.

I was sitting on the bench outside Burgh's heart-
burn-haven when Jean Northenor, organizer of the
Republican underground and chairperson of the
Margaret Thatcher Fan Club, came waltzing up the
sidewalk.

"Jean, why do you suppose fishermen wear hats?"
I asked with appropriate respect.

"Because," she responded with papal-like authority while raising her fist into the air.

That, friends, I can live with.

Bureaucrats at Work

Your Tax Dollars at Work

Melvin Mossback is just your average Chapman Lake beaver doing what all beavers do each fall — build a dam and a lodge.

He and his wife, Rosebud, along with the three kits (no, it's not "kids") Philo, Herman and Barney were busily engaged in tree cutting, bark stripping and mud packing when two well-dressed agents from the Army Corps of Engineers (ACE) and the Indiana Department of Environmental Management (IDEM) showed up.

"Are you Melvin Mossback, the beaver?" one agent asked in authoritative tones.

"That I am," Melvin said proudly as he stood next to his nearly-completed dam. "What can I do for you?"

"Have you filed forms DD3-7 and HTF-227 and do you have a permit to construct this dam?" he demanded while snapping pictures of the structure.

"Why should I file any forms?" Melvin responded

with surprise. "My family has been building dams here for generations, and none of them had permits. In fact, we were building dams in this area hundreds of years before there even was an Army Corps of Engineers."

"Well, I'm afraid you are not in compliance with regulations HR-662, BT-913 and CCR-221-7A, and I will have to cite you. There will be some penalties, of course."

"Are you aware that your dam is flooding a large area upstream?" T.J. Trashbloom of IDEM asked.

"Of course I am, that's why beavers build dams," Melvin noted. "Then waterfowl can nest, fish can spawn, and Paul Miller can play with his rubber ducky in the backyard."

Melvin and Rosebud were just about to go into their lodge when a government boat pulled up and three inspectors from the Indiana Department of Labor (IDL) and two from the Occupational Safety and Health Administration (OSHA) jumped out, cameras and notebooks in hand.

"Are you Mossback, Melvin, J. SS No. 16-6345-224?" the OSHA inspector shouted so all the busy beavers within two miles could hear.

"I am and what do you want?" Melvin replied as Philo, Herman and Barney joined him next to the dam.

"Have you provided all your employees with a Haz-Comm. Program and proper MSDS's in compliance with Title 29, Subpart D, Part 1926.59, and if not, why not?" the senior inspector demanded.

"I don't even know what the devil those things are," Melvin replied as his fur began to bristle with irritation.

"Haz-Comm. is the government's Hazard Communication Program to make sure that all chemicals on your site are evaluated and that your employees know the dangers, and MSDS's are the Material Safety Data Sheets that must be available for all chemicals used at the site," the inspector explained.

"We beavers don't use any hazardous material to build our dams and lodges, only natural things like sticks, mud, bark and sometimes corn stalks if they are nearby," Melvin retorted.

"If that's so," the Inspector argued, "what is this can of WD-40 oil doing next to the shore? Do you have a MSDS for this, and is it posted not less than three feet but not more than five feet above the ground as required by Statute 999-275-BBF? If not, you are in violation of Job Site Regulation CFR 332-8524-771-B and are subject to a $5,000 fine."

"No, I don't have a MSDS for that oil," Melvin snapped back. "That can of oil floated up on shore three months before we began the dam and has nothing to do with our work."

"I'm sorry, that dangerous material is on your construction site and without a MSDS you are harboring an unidentified hazardous substance in violation of Code HB-223-R-775-290-Z and Section 7 of Code BBR-65-SAT. That'll be another $5,000."

By this time the whole family stood in shock as the inspectors took measurements of the dam and the lodge. One man collected samples of the mud and sticks and carefully placed them in lab bags for further testing.

The youngest of the OSHA inspectors, Fred Farleft, opened his five-inch notebook and shouted in monarchical tones, "You are building a structure on public land, Mossback. Are you a licensed engineer and do you have a proper degree from MIT to undertake such a project?"

"I don't need all that," Melvin responded angrily. "I've built dams and lodges for 10 years and not one has failed or broken. We beavers know about things like that without exams, textbooks, professors, football games and fraternity houses."

"I don't see any entrance to your place of dwelling," Hector Hardright of OSHA shouted as he stood on the top of Melvin's lodge. "How do you get in and out of this thing anyway?"

"There's only one entrance and it's underwater," Rosebud answered. "That way we have good protection from predators when we need to escape them."

"Oh no, that won't do," the inspector grumbled as he shook his head in disbelief. "Somebody could drown attempting to get in or out of the lodge in an emergency. Besides, it's in violation of OSHA Reg. 113, 114, 115 and 772-Domestic Egress and Entrance."

"But beavers know how to swim from birth—it's natural—and the underwater entrance keeps dogs and other animals from catching us," she explained as twinges of anger now turned to waves of fury.

"We're very sorry, Mr. and Mrs. Mossback, but we are issuing a cease-and-desist order on dam construction here, and the OSHA, IDEM, IDL and ACE violations will cost you $143,567 in fines and penalties," the OSHA inspector announced.

"Of course, if you want to appeal, you can come to Indianapolis, St. Louis, and Washington D.C. with your attorney and maybe some of those fines can be reduced. We government people are very understanding and sympathetic, you know."

"In the meantime, however, we are required by law to arrest you and place all of you in jail until bail can be arranged and a trial date set."

Isn't it good to know that your tax dollars are at work?

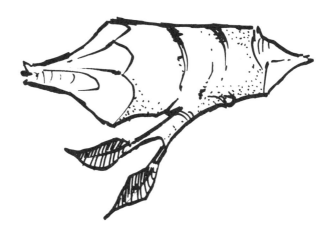

Fishing Is Pure Excitement

The Greatest Sport

All things considered, I'd rather be fishing.

I reached that profound conclusion having meticulously scrutinized all of life's most significant alternatives over a rather lengthy period of time.

My friend, Achish Featherbelt, keeps mumbling something about the glories of baseball as the perfect pastime, but whenever I go to see the Cubs, I get severe heartburn from both the hot dogs and the score.

Barry Bulrush, a magician with a golf club, insists that golf is the game of games. I tried it once and my game was so astounding that halfway around the course all the flags flew at half-mast and every squirrel within three miles had donned a helmet. I spent an inordinate amount of time fishing my golf balls out of the water, and when I filleted them later, there was hardly anything left for the frying pan.

Furthermore, I have serious misgivings about any sport where the guy with the highest score loses.

Water skiing has been touted by Harvy Moot as the greatest of sports, but I don't get very excited about being scraped off somebody's seawall with a putty knife.

I also don't want to hear about the benefits of tennis. Running around in your underwear while hitting a ball across a net does not strike me as a significant activity.

You get all sweaty and have to take a shower. Everybody knows how inconvenient that can be when you get past two or three showers a year. Besides, nets were made for fishing, not for banging fuzzy balls over.

Dr. Samuel Walkabit argues quite ardently that doing yard work is a man's most relaxing and rewarding activity. But with all due respect, if he feels that getting cut by thorn bushes, bitten by mosquitoes, stung by bees and hollered at by the neighbor for using smelly fertilizer is entertainment, his mental gears must be in neutral.

Cutting the lawn is nothing more than botanical brutality. Grass was meant to grow and to deny it this very fundamental plant right is to flirt with ecological disaster. Mowing one's lawn is not sport, entertainment or an act of beautification . . . it is a wanton destruction of the vital green pigments nature provides to photosynthetic organisms.

Where does Dr. Walkabit think worms and grubs will find sanctuary if he chops innocent blades of grass off in the prime of life? Besides, nesting quail need high grass and deer dance in it!

No, my friends, the above recreational activities are only o.k. if you're really old and decrepit, and there is no lake, pond, stream or river within 100 miles of your home. Barring such decrepitude, how-

ever, fishing was and always will be the most rewarding of recreational activities.

It is above all, educational. You will learn, for
example, that skunks will raise a stink if you should
cover their hole with a cooler or tackle box while
fishing from a bank. You also learn that virtually all
rental boats leak and at least half the nightcrawlers
you buy in a small container are dead.

Furthermore, fishing is exciting. I can remember
well having the front of my kayak aerated by a duck
hunter on little Chapman Lake some years ago.
Then, there was the time I sat down on a plug with
three treble hooks on it. The dance I did for the next
ten minutes brought four days of rain to Indiana!

Don't forget the thrill of glancing up after you
have unloaded your boat in the water and seeing the
drain plug sitting on the deck.

Fishing offers many holistic health benefits, as
well. You learn to be an early riser and develop
unusual patience in the face of total nonproductivity.
Sun, wind and rain tan and age your face so that by
age 20 you are widely sought after for old hunting
and fishing stories.

In addition, the fruit of your fishing labors, the
fish dinners, are thoroughly enriching. Not only, for
example, do the Chicago River filets glow in the
dark, but with every six ounces of meat you get your
daily requirements of DDT's, PCB's and mercury.

Finally, don't forget the sheer serenity that comes
with pulling weeds off your spinner bait and forget-
ting there is a trailer hook, or the calm that surrounds
you as your wife slams the trunk lid on your brand new,
$425 super boron, custom-made baitcasting rod.

Yep! I'm convinced. All things considered and
weighed . . . I'd rather be fishing.

Neckties: Handicaps to Self Defense

Neckties are
the Problem

Surely, you have given some thought to the tensions and troubles which exist in our present world. Tempers flare, cannons blast homes apart, and congressmen scream at the Contra hearings.

What has made our world such a noisy, nasty mess? Immediately, some will point to radically different philosophies that influence men's actions. Others will cite economic factors or military threats as the explanation for such insane behavior. But these folks are all wrong.

Neckties are the problem.

As a keenly observant outdoor writer I should have noticed this long ago. Whenever I've gone into the beautiful forests and fished on glassy lakes, I always feel a sense of release, relaxation and refreshment.

My inclination has been to attribute this emotional and psychological ecstasy to fresh air and quiet landscapes.

Wrong!

It was all due to the fact that I did not have a necktie on.

The scientific explanation for this was recently published by a group of scholars at Cornell University; they concluded, after lengthy studies, that neckties (especially when tied tight) reduce blood circulation to the brain thus distorting judgment, giving the wearer headaches and impairing vision.

Think about it for a moment. Did you ever see a groundhog shoot his brother-in-law or a possum steal his neighbor's TV set? Of course not, they don't wear ties and their good judgment is not hindered.

Last evening I watched network news and saw warlike threats hurled back and forth by two national leaders. Both were wearing neckties.

The missile reduction talks between Russian and American representatives are badly bogged down, but that is understandable. They all wear tight-fitting neckties during the long hours of tedious negotiation so blood circulation must only trickle to their brains.

Neckties are also a scourge to family relations. Your favorite mother-in-law buys you a solid purple tie with large green polka dots for Christmas, and your wife demands that you wear it with your light tan suit when you go to church on Sunday. There's no way you can come out a winner on that one.

If you wear the thing, you will be laughed right out of the balcony, but if you refuse, dear wife and mom will establish a two-person war department.

Ties are also hazardous to working people. How many men have had their noses rearranged because their tie got caught in a piece of machinery?

My Arab friend, Helmi Musa, once suggested

that neckties are the cause of baldness among men. He insists, "my people have no problems with baldness because most of the men do not wear ties."

Have you noticed that very few ladies are bald? The reason is quite elementary; they get good circulation to the head because they are not choked by a gaudy cloth around their necks.

I was reared in the shadow of South Philadelphia where, early in life, I learned the impracticality of a tie. When a good street rumble broke out, I didn't want to give some slob a handle to get to my nose.

Did you ever notice how many times in the movies one of Al Capone's men would grab the tie of some poor guy before handing him a knuckleburger? Ties are despicable handicaps to good self defense.

I am now convinced that neckties are also a serious social and economic inconvenience. Styles keep changing back and forth from long, slim types to wide, gaudy numbers. The price of some ties is downright scandalous. One store in Chicago wanted $50 for a tie! Think of it. Paying fifty smackeroos just to have the blood circulation to your brain cut off.

According to the Neckwear Association of America, the tie is the number one seller for Father's Day. Of course, you'd expect them to say that. But have we really done ol' dad a favor buying him a cloth contraption that will impair even more his already failing circulatory system?

I wanted to learn something of the origin of the necktie, so I talked to ol' Cory Clingtight who has been in the clothing business since the turn of the century.

"Yeah, I remember how that necktie business all got started," he said as he lit his pipe. "The boys were

fixin' to hang a guy in Dusty Gulch, Wyoming, when ·
a judge came storming up on a horse and demanded
the man be cut down because he was innocent."

"Well, the man had only been hanging a few
seconds, so they cut the red rope about 12 inches
above his head, and when he stood on the wooden
platform, the noose dropped down on his light blue
shirt and the combination was downright striking."

"Within days the local tailor, Thorndike
Thistlefoot, had half the men wearing red ties. The
rest is history."

The thing that really clinches the issue for me,
however, is the fact that many of the world's greatest
thinkers never wore ties. Einstein, Plato, Augustine
did not wear ties! They were men of philosophical
distinction and acute insight, and they refused to
lynch themselves for fashion. So why should the rest
of us?

Then, too, have you ever noticed how virtually
all politicians wear ties.

I wonder how tight those things are?

The Waiting Game

My First Duck

When I finally came to the brutal realization that I had peaked socially and intellectually at age six, I understood why most of my childhood memories were either a blur or lost altogether.

The memory of shooting my first wild duck, however, remains safely etched on what little gray matter has managed to survive the ravages of time.

I was reared in south Jersey where abundant streams and swamps provided the perfect habitats for gigantic mosquitoes which regularly flew in formation during their search for corpuscles both red and white.

The hot, muggy, mosquito-filled summer days were spent working on old man Glover's farm picking cucumbers and tomatoes for wages that would have sent a union chief into a complete frenzy. The income, modest as it was, did eventually enable me to purchase my first shotgun, a Savage, 20 gauge single shot.

But the real goal of that year was to be ready for duck hunting season and a chance at some of the thousands of black ducks which made their way south along the south Jersey shoreline. "But how can you even think of serious duck hunting without a dog?" I asked myself.

I'm very glad I was listening at the time, for it wasn't long after that I snookered my parents into buying me an English setter. "This dog will be able to do it all," I gurgled with confidence. "When my training program is through, he will be able to point to pheasants, quail and grouse in the field and retrieve downed ducks from the river."

My father shook his head in acknowledgment, but the smile on his face left me a little uneasy.

So how do you train a high-strung English setter for serious hunting? That's easy, you take him out in the field and first introduce him to your shotgun.

My dog, Topper, was really ready to go hunting when I got home from school, so I grabbed the gun and headed toward the woods behind my house. "Topper," I said assuringly, "this thing might be a little noisy at first, but you'll get used to it."

With that brief introduction, I shot into the air and Topper, who was facing east at the time jumped three feet straight up and landed facing west. In seconds his little paws had taken him over the fence and up to the back door of the house.

My mother, who was doubled over with laughter, hung on to the screen door to keep her footing and mercifully let the trembling mutt in the house.

That whole mess crippled my ego a mite, but did not diminish my desire for the hunt.

With all the excitement, however, my mother failed to notice that Topper, who was now in the final stages of panic recovery, had committed an act of indiscretion on the new living room rug.

Suddenly the smiles and snickers disappeared.

My father, who was now madder than a skunk in a bees' nest, mumbled something about glue factories taking dogs as well as old horses.

Well, Topper and I survived that rather shaky start and continued to pursue hunting careers. I bought some old, beat-up decoys from a river rat named "Skins," so Topper and I could attract crowds of ducks to our "deadly" duck blind.

Half the heads were missing, but I figured that it wasn't a serious problem since it was rumored that most of the ducks in the area had bad eyesight anyway.

My friend, Ralph, and I carted my canvas kayak to Big Timber Creek (a branch of the Delaware River near Camden) and paddled our way to the duck blind with Topper serving as a front seat navigator.

After setting the decoys, we loaded our guns and waited for the sun to rise and the action to begin. "You take the first shot, Ralph, " I said while shivering in the light rain that had just begun. "If there is more than one, I'll take whatever trails."

Sure enough, a lone mallard came quacking around the bend at a 50 mile an hour clip and Ralph let go with his father's single shot, 12 gauge, 34-inch artillery piece. Not one feather dropped from the duck, Ralph was knocked over by the recoil from the gun and Topper having cleared the wall of cattails around the blind, was nowhere to be seen.

This was certainly not what I had dreamed about the night before!

Shortly, I got my turn when a much smaller duck soared above the decoys. My gun rang out. The duck dropped in the muck that now appeared between the duck blind and the river.

We had forgotten that the tide was dropping and soon discovered that the kayak would no longer float! Topper, the trusty retriever was gone, so I was forced to climb out of the blind and slosh my way to the duck. "Funny looking duck," I shouted to Ralph. "It's all black and has a beak like a crow."

"That's a coot. You shot a dumb ol' coot," Ralph chuckled.

"It doesn't matter. It's something and it beats your nothing all to pieces. I'm taking it home," I shouted defiantly.

It was near noon by the time we got the kayak through the chemical-laden muck of that old river and finally arrived home. By then the coot smelled something awful.

"Well, here it is," I chirped proudly as I held the mangy thing high so my mother, who was in the other side of the kitchen, could see it. "This is going to make a great meal for the family."

"What is that thing?" she shouted in total dismay.

"It's a coot. They live on the water with the ducks. It was roaring along at 90 miles per hour when I hit it. One shot, that's all it took for ol' eagle-eye," I bragged.

I could tell she was not caught up in the excitement of the moment. She pondered the whole situation and finally spoke. "Y'know the ancient Indians, who used to live in this area, had a sacred tradition of burying the first duck they got each season to bring good luck. Maybe you should do that so you will get many more during the season."

That sure made sense to me. I immediately went to the garden in the back yard and gave the thing a proper ceremonial burial.

I never cease to be amazed at the insight mothers have into Indian lore, outdoor mysteries, woodland traditions and things like that.

The Art of Making Verbal Noise

What Did He Say?

The conversation was fairly normal at the back table of Heartburn Haven.

Willie Woodchip, Buddy Splitshot, Archie Adenoid and Hector Hackshot covered a wide range of topics as they scraped the charcoal off the toast and sipped what was billed as coffee, but had the bite of battery acid.

As Bill Backlash approached the table, he was asked how the fishing was on Winona Lake.

"If'n ya really want to know, we slithered out to the slosh at the south end 'n slaughtered some hungry hawgs by doodle sockin' in the winders," was the reply.

"What did he say?" Willie asked in total bewilderment.

"Well, if I get the drift correctly, he said he caught some large, aggressive bass in the thick weed beds at the south end of the lake by flipping jigs through the small openings," Arnie offered.

The response of Bill Backlash is typical of a rapidly growing fraternity whose conversation is normally understandable, but who, when fishing is discussed, produced flow of verbal gobbledegook. "Hawg" (hog) is a favorite reference to a large bass which is replacing "lunker." In fact, if you are younger than 45, you are likely to use "hawg" while those anglers older than 45 will usually choose "lunker."

The impact of bass clubs, tournaments and magazines has had a significant influence on the younger fisherman.

To "slaughter" a fish is to catch a large number. The term is borrowed from the record of General Custer's performance at Little Big Horn and that of the Chicago Bears when playing the Washington Redskins.

"Doodle-sockin'" is a more recent expression referring to the a form of jigging by means of which the lure is flipped into under water brush, lily pads or some other type of cover.

And then there are the clichés. While fishermen are guilty of repeating those thread-bare ambiguities, politicians are the world's worst offenders.

Most current political speeches are saturated with an irritating number of words that no longer mean anything definite at all. They have been reduced to mere verbal noises.

Words like "progressive," "liberal," "conservative," "bourgeois," "militant," "middle-class," "fiscally responsible," and "balanced budget" have been twisted beyond recognition.

Notice how this excerpt from a political speech snows you into speechlessness.

"I want to be perfectly clear on the issue of finance. It is my firm conviction that community needs can only be considered on an annual basis if and when budgetary priorities are evaluated against fiscally sound proposals providing, of course, that tax revenues rise up to or are in excess of normal expectations," economist Sam Stockdown announced.

An elderly lady leaned across the table and asked, "What did he say?"

Of course, specificity in public speeches is not highly desirable if the politician is attempting to stand firmly in mid- air, on both sides of an issue.

A slip of the tongue in a recent speech proved to be more revealing than the entire rest of the speech. A new candidate, emphasizing his personal honesty and deep desire to hold office, stated with gusto, "I have never stolen anything in my life. All I ask is a chance." The lack of pause between sentences was disastrous.

Everyday the American public is bombarded with such empty expressions as "viable objectives," "fruitful dialogue" and "meaningful exchanges."

Proposals by the political opposition are always "totally unacceptable," "unresponsive to the legitimate aspirations of the people," or "superficial."

I am still trying to envisage the notion of a "think-tank." Is that a large pool where disembodied intellectuals float around in search of ideas?

Political conversations are filled with "credibility gaps," "affordable alternatives," "relevant prospects," and "significant progress." Of course, politicians do need to express themselves with great care. More than one speaker has opened his mouth and had a foot fall out.

One of the more controversial twists in verbal communication has come about as a result of feminist demands. In order to eliminate "sexploitation," we now have "chairpersons," "milkpersons," and "fisherpersons," ("anglerettes?") which are each regarded as a victory for "personkind."

Remember all the brouhaha over the degeneration of the language resulting from teenage banter? Teens have given us such wonderful innovations such as "cool," "square," "with it," "swinger," "jive," "far out," "y'know," and the more recent, "in your face," and "no way."

Attend any one of the 10 million annual seminars on business success and you will be overrun with words like "sensitivity," "consensus," "interface," "logistics," "bottom line," "charismatic," "relevant" and "productive."

If I hear "prioritize" or "bottom line" at one more seminar, I may scream.

It is difficult to determine if the sterilization of words is the result of verbal sloppiness or vogue-word innovation. Clearly, many words are selected to impress the hearer rather than to communicate the speaker's thoughts.

The decline in language purity has caught the attention of none other than his royal highness, Prince Philip, who recently listed "macho," "charismatic," "avant garde," "nihilism" and "upcoming" as words with an ugsome meaning.

"Ugsome?"

Yep. I checked an unabridged *Oxford English Dictionary* and found that this principally Scottish word means, "horrible."

Joining Prince Philip are a growing number of scholars and others who have appointed themselves as guardians of the English language. The ol' scribe is not among them, however.

The English language has gone through change in every century of its existence and the dynamics of that change are as fascinating as the people who created them. I firmly believe it will continue to survive whatever inanities we can throw its way.

Well, as I look at the clock on the wall, it appears that it is time to cease this wandering meditation and go fishing.

If'n y'all don't mind, I think I'll mosey out to my boat with a handful of minnies and pound the H_2O for some hungry hawgs. I hear they are a sloshin' around the garbage at the south end of Winona Lake. If I can just doodle-sock a few through the winders, I bet I'll slaughter a bunch.

Johann Strauss at Work

A Famous
Carp Fisherman

It was an unusually beautiful day as Franz Adorno and I drifted down the historic Danube River in Vienna during the summer of 1984.

Large trees along its mysterious banks produced eerie shadows upon the water which has for centuries reflected images of Vienna's ancient buildings.

The only thoroughly disturbing part of that memorable journey was my observation that the Danube — contrary to the musical observations of Johann Strauss — was not "blue." In fact, it was dirty, muddy and featured a variety of floating debris that Franz was able to date back to the 70's.

Strauss (1825-1899), also known as "king of the waltz," has given the world some of the greatest music scores ever penned, and The Blue Danube is among them.

"But why would he call the Danube 'blue' when it has eternally been a brown, sediment-laden river?" I asked Franz.

65

"We Austrians like to indulge ourselves in musical fantasies to escape the harsh realities of life," Franz explained with university eloquence. "Johann Strauss was acclaimed everywhere as Austria's most successful ambassador, and it was incumbent upon him to present the Danube in a way that would increase tourism, which in turn, helped to finance the fine arts in the city."

I was intrigued with Franz's reply, but also convinced that it didn't really get to the issue.

Music historians like to refer to Strauss' "chronic ailment" as an explanation for his sometimes exotic language and behavior. I thought perhaps this might explain the issue of his intentional color distortion.

Conventional wisdom identifies his problem as an acute abdominal distress, but Franz was clearly unwilling to buy that since he too drank the city's water and had no problems.

In an effort to resolve the hydrologic contradiction raised by Strauss' Blue Danube waltz, I went to Warsaw's official center for culture and learning: Breadings' Cigar Store. Fortunately, philosopher, historian, political pundit and Chef-in-Residence, Professor Burleigh Burgh, DDT, PCB, ATT, was there and poised to resolve any dilemma known to man.

"Burleigh, why did Johann Strauss call the Danube River 'blue' in his famous waltz when everybody in Vienna knew it was brown, grey or green?"

"That's easy, John, m'boy," Burgh replied with an Oxford-like confidence. "Johann Strauss hallucinated while composing the piece due to a serious overdose of canned Vienna Sausage and sauerkraut consumed during lunch."

The large group of scholastics gathered around the domino tables broke into a thunderous applause at what they perceived to be a staggeringly brilliant historic and scientific analysis of an infrequently considered problem.

I, however, was compelled to reject that theory since there is not one scrap of evidence Strauss ever ate the stuff and, furthermore, it's a matter of history that the Viennese did not start canning sausage until 1922, long after his death.

It was while I was sitting along the banks of the Tippicanoe River with a carp fishermen that the solution to my nagging musical problem came to me.

The Tippi was very high and muddy since it had rained hard the day before, but that did not discourage my friend, Hiram Hackwood, from going after some big carp.

"How is the river today?" I asked as Hiram put a blob of worms on his hook.

"It's blue and beautiful," he replied with a glow on his deeply lined face.

Mud and debris floated by at the very moment Hiram was extolling the aesthetic and piscatorial virtues of the Tippicanoe.

"That's it!" I said to myself. "Johann Strauss was a carp fishermen, and like all carp anglers, he saw only blue and beautiful rivers."

Just this morning before nudging up to my computer to write this article I pulled out a compact disk and played with perfect peace of mind and serenity of soul, the beautiful Blue Danube waltz.

Now that I have unraveled this great mystery, carp fishermen world-wide can thoroughly enjoy the majestic music written by one of their own.

Praying Mantis

Moth

Cockroach

Japanese Beetle

Mosquito

Ladybug

The Cockroach: King of The Bugs

Official City Bug

How long, oh, how long will the city of Warsaw remain in the backwash of cultural obscurity?

While the great cities of Indiana like Claypool, Packerton and Leesburg march ahead with innovative plans to achieve notoriety, our town lies dead in the water.

Sure, Warsaw finally got its own fruit festival, but that comes decades after Plymouth has celebrated the blueberry festival, Packerton its fig festival and Claypool the prune festival (the population of Claypool is a bit older than most cities).

While the Warsaw Common Council squabbles over such inconsequential issues as holes in the roads, a new athletic complex, the new high school and expansion of route 15, other cities are entering the 1990's with a fish flying on their flags and vegetables on their logos.

Years ago I pleaded with the Mayor of our city to declare the majestic asparagus the official city vegetable. Noting the unique qualities of this magnificent vegetable, I argued that Warsaw could lead the nation in cultural innovation.

Our highest elected official snubbed my humble suggestion, and since then the United States Congress has designated an entire month as National Asparagus Month. How humiliating it is to have the world's largest debate society outsmart our municipal officials.

Later, I called the unique and exquisite qualities of the carp to the Mayor's attention and suggested that he establish it as the official city fish. Once again I was summarily ignored.

Now I have it on good authority that no less than 23 cities in the US have adopted various fish as their official symbols, including the carp! I cried all night over that one.

Most journalists would have given up by now assuming that their city was doomed to perpetual cultural obscurantism, but not the ol' scribe. I might not be smart, but I am persistent.

I just can't sit around doing nothing while our citizens suffer social and cultural depression, to say nothing of political embarrassment.

It seems to me that Warsaw could quickly join the ranks of the truly creative towns if it had an official city bug. At the present time, there's not one city in our nation that has adopted a bug as its official city symbol.

Most cities have an official flower, bird, or animal, but none has demonstrated the entomological foresight to name a bug as its symbol.

In order to get a good handle on this thing, I decided to interview several of Warsaw's most prominent intellectuals and social leaders.

The logical place to find the largest concentrations of these individuals was in that hotbed of scholasticism and political profundity ... Breadings' Cigar Store.

"An official city bug?" Corey Clingtight asked. "Hey, man, that's cool and like I think the candidate should be the mischievous mosquito. Mosquitoes are like common to our area and like really know how to get your attention. Like this is an honor they like justly deserve."

"Dat's a crock o' baloney," Barry Bushrack shouted. "Der am only one true bug dat would make Warsaw a fittin' symbol ... da moth. Dem tings can buzz a light at 50 miles an hour and smash into a lit bulb at full tilt and never git a headache. Dey's good eaters, too."

Everyone's attention was now focused on the back table as Warsaw's finest minds debated the ins and outs of this profound and culturally critical issue.

Rev. Wilber Walkright decided to offer his opinion. (The Rev. feels strongly that he was called to evangelize pagans and since Breadings' has the largest collection of them, he spends considerable time there).

"Thou art all amiss on this one, my children," he noted. "Considering the religious and spiritual legacy of our area, the only bug that makes sense for a symbol is the praying mantis. This bug sets a most favorable example for all of us, and since our Mayor is not an atheist, the choice should be easy."

"Not so fast, Reverend. I can understand your choice, but you've got to broaden your horizons on this issue. What we have here is the need for a symbol with contemporary political and economic significance," Fred Flylight, Warsaw's international trade tycoon, chimed in. "In light of current trends in investment, manufacturing and the acquisition of American real estate the choice should be the Japanese Beetle."

"They really have made progress in our country. In 1916 only a few were found on some plants in New Jersey; now there are millions all over the northeast and midwest. They represent growth, innovation and durability."

As the conversation heated up, master chef, Burleigh Burgh kept the cups filled with his best black brew. It has been a long-standing practice to keep Breadings' customers arguing over controversial issues so they would not think about the food they were eating.

Bees, ants, crickets, and grasshoppers were all nominated by the back table gang. I could see, however, that we were not reaching anything that resembled a consensus (a regular occurrence in Breadings'), so I rambled outside somewhat depressed and sat on the city bench.

Marching briskly up the pavement with a large bank ledger in her hand was the county's Republican guru (gurette?), Jean Northenor.

"Jean, I'm having a difficult time getting a consensus on what Warsaw's official bug should be," I said in somber tones. "Can you give me some help?"

"John, m'boy, you've come to the right place. We lady Republicans are big on bugs. If you take numbers, beauty and sheer intellect, the only choice would have to be the lady bug," she chirped with bubbling enthusiasm.

"They're colorful, smart and tough as nails. What better symbol could we have than the lofty lady bug?

Margaret Thatcher has one mounted on her desk, and Barbara Bush is planning to use it as a wall pattern in her home in Kennebunkport, Maine," she concluded.

I never should have asked.

Time was slipping by and I could just see Fort Wayne or South Bend beating us to this important choice. I couldn't bear to see Warsaw endure another year of social and cultural ignominy without an official symbol.

At my moment of deepest frustration and with my notebook still empty, Burleigh Burgh emerged from his food emporium after a hard day of three-hours work (he runs his own union).

"Burleigh, I didn't hear anything from you while the men were debating a choice for Warsaw's official bug. What do you think?" I asked.

Taking his St. Louis Cardinals baseball cap off (he is still deeply committed to minor league baseball), he sat down and with two words put his staggering intellect and insightful wisdom on display.

"The cockroach," he announced with authority.

"Warsaw must have a bug that has some stature, genius, and toughness. Only the cockroach fills the bill. I have dealt with the little monsters for years in my professional activities, and I find them most impressive."

"They can get big and are clearly intimidating. I remember when Smitty shouted up from the basement that there was a big cockroach down there. 'Smash the thing with your shoe,' I hollered. 'I can't. It's wearing my shoe' he shouted back."

"Now that, John, is a big cockroach. Yep, that rascal is well-represented here in Warsaw and would make a great official bug."

I found myself unable to ignore such amazing and irrefutable logic. "That's it," I said to myself. "The cockroach could be Warsaw's official bug.

My spirit was lifted as a flood of ideas drifted into the harbors of my mind.

I could see a large cockroach flying proudly on the flag over city hall. We could then remove those silly and archaic shields from the police cars and have an angry cockroach standing there instead. Just think, truck drivers across America would all be talking about Warsaw. Perhaps they would even salute as one of Warsaw's finest drove past them on Route 30; it would be glorious!

Mr. Mayor, I know your political career has slipped a little into the muck of municipal obscurity. But I want you and our city to become household words in America and here is the perfect chance to make it all happen.

Make the magnificent cockroach the official bug of our city and you will be the talk of the state . . . maybe even the nation.

The economic impact will be enormous. In all likelihood, Black Flag Corporation will relocate their international headquarters here, and the Fly Swatter Manufacturing Association will move all their operations to the Route 30 industrial corridor.

Hundreds of jobs will be created, and Warsaw will take its rightful place as a hotbed of cultural innovation.

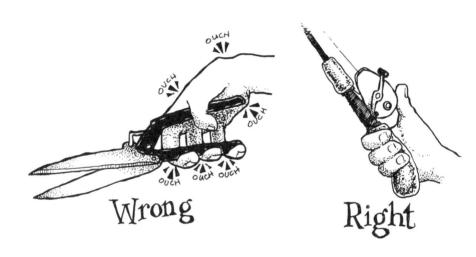

Wrong

Right

A Man's Hand Was Made for Fishing

It's a Matter
of Biology

Did you ever notice how nicely a man's hand fits around the handle of a fishing rod?

That's no accident, of course.

In fact, intensive research in the fields of biology and human osteology have led me to the unchallengeable conclusion that a man's hand is purposely structured for such things as fishing rods, golf clubs and baseball bats.

On the other hand, it is equally amazing how perfectly a woman's hand fits brooms, frying pans and vacuum cleaners.

Elated with this significant discovery, I decided to share the information with my wife during lunch.

"Honey, do you know what a fisherman is?" I asked as a subtle introduction to the subject.

"Sure," she responded authoritatively, "It's a jerk at one end of the line waiting for a jerk at the other end."

My keen journalistic instincts told me that this

was not going to be an easy task, but every husband is obligated to share important news with his wife.

"No, it is a man maximizing the metacarpal and phalangeal uses of his hand for productive enterprises," I observed with appropriate dignity. "Furthermore, the very size of those bones is perfect for such strenuous activities as hunting and fishing."

"Funny thing," she responded, "I always thought the larger size was designed to aid a man in carrying the garbage from the house to the street."

It was obvious, at this point, that the osteological data I presented had not made a significant impact, so I decided to shift to statistical information.

"I was just thinking the other day that since 3/4 of the earth's surface is water and only 1/4 land, men should be spending 3/4 of their time fishing and only 1/4 working."

"Would you like mustard or mayonnaise on your sandwich?" she asked, obviously ignoring the irrefutable logic of my argument.

Now that she was weakening in the face of weighty dialogue and impeccable reasoning, I decided to pop the all-important question. "Do you mind if I do a little fishing this afternoon?"

"Well, I had hoped you would take your superior metacarpals, humeri and ulna bones and wrap them around the clippers in order to get the bushes trimmed," she quipped with icy sarcasm.

"Now, there we have a serious biological problem. First, the muscular action required for clipping is unnatural and second, the result of such barbarous activity butchers the natural habitat for little birds. You wouldn't want me to deprive those little creatures of proper shade and food, would you?"

By this time we had left the table, and I had

spread my tackle on the living room floor in anticipation of the afternoon fishing trip.

"As long as you're doing nothing, why don't you go outside and cut the grass before it rains tonight?" she asked.

"But I am not doing nothing. I am doing something," I asserted. "Arranging tackle is something."

"Well, it's next to nothing. Besides the grass has grown so tall that giraffes and elephants have moved in," she added.

"It's biologically unsound to cut grass too often," I observed with cold logic. "In the hot weather short grass will quickly burn up and with the loss of surface moisture, we will lose all our nightcrawlers."

Now, with growing confidence, I pressed on with my arguments for fishing as man's natural enterprise.

"Aside from the biological and structural features of man's body that make him suitable for fishing, there are the psychological factors. Something inside him yearns for the outdoors with its splendorously varied landscapes, the invigorating benefits of fresh air and the joy that comes with the catch."

Lifting my voice to capture just the right tone of authority I announced, "these hands were made for water."

"Well, that's just marvelous," she responded with a disconcerting sense of joy. "There's a pile of dishes in the sink and a nice large pail of water, too. Your hands will be delighted. I'm going to the women's meeting." With that she gleefully stepped out the front door.

Wives just don't understand biology.

Government Bureaucrat	**Common Citizen**

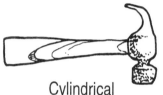

Cylindrical
High-Impact Instrument

Hammer

Diversified
Torque Implement

Screwdriver

Bi-Sectional
Incisor Component

Two-Bladed Knife

Government Gobbledegook

Surely you've read those ads that go, "Government surplus sale. Jeeps for dollars. Knives, tools and domestic items for only cents."

One such ad recently caught the eye of my fishing buddy, Thorndike Waterlog, so he decided to write and order a surplus hammer, screwdriver, and knife. Three months later he received his order back along with the check and a large red stamp that read, "Improper Procurement Statement."

He couldn't imagine what the problem might have been because he took the time to type the order and double check his addition.

"Why don't you ask ol' Barry Bushrack, Procurement Specialist for the Pentagon, what that stamp means,?" I suggested. "He used to live here in Warsaw and was a regular guy who got heartburn at Breadings' Cigar Store like everyone else. Surely, he could help."

It took dialing five offices in Washington, D.C.

before Barry's voice was heard on the other end of the line. "This is Bushrack, Section I-A of the Purchase and Procurement Division, Government Surplus, Sector One."

"Hi, Barry. This is your ol' friend, Thorndike Waterlog here in Warsaw, and I was wondering why my order for a surplus hammer, screwdriver and knife was sent back from your division stamped, 'Improper Procurement Statement?'"

"Let me find your order on our new SX-1Q Systems Recall Smacko-Data computer complex. Ah, here it is! We rejected your procurement proposition for lack of verbal clarity."

"What verbal clarity?" Thorndike snapped with irritation. "I asked for a hammer, screwdriver and a knife. What could be clearer?"

"Sorry, Thorndike, the government does not recognize "hammer." It is a cylindrical high impact instrument. We can't fulfill procurement requests that are semantically incorrect or ambiguous."

"Look, I remember when you asked to borrow three different screwdrivers from me when we were building a chicken coop in Claypool. So what do you call them now?" Thorndike wanted to know.

"Purchase of different sized surplus screwdrivers will require that you ask for diversified torque implements."

Now, friends, Thorndike is normally a calm, well-adjusted man, but government gobbledegook was wearing his patience thin. At stake here was a total of $3.25 worth of surplus merchandise, and conventional federal wisdom was turning the whole mess into a verbal nightmare.

"I'll tell you before you ask; one no longer asks for a two bladed knife. It is a bi-sectioned incisor instrument. You surely can see how simple the government has made things by using clear, accurate and precise language," Bushrack bragged.

"By the way, Thorndike, you will be delighted to know that we just received 13,000 surplus bathtubs from the army. They cost $4,000 each originally, but you can order one for just $9.98."

"Hey, that sounds like a great idea, Barry; put me down for one of those bathtubs," Thorndike gurgled.

"Sorry, we do not officially stock surplus bathtubs, they are known as personal aquatic containment units."

Thorndike's patience ran out with that last bit of nonsense so he shouted over the phone, "forget the whole order, Barry; I'll wait for the next local garage sale for tool bargains. At least they'll speak plain English there."

"Listen, Thorndike, I understand you're coming down here to Washington, D.C. on business. How about if you and I go out to dinner?" Bushrack asked.

"Great idea, Barry. I'll see you at six o'clock in the Pentagon dining commons."

"Now, before you get away, Thorndike, let me write this meeting down so I won't forget. 'Meet Thorndike at Pentagon organic supply center at 1800 hours for a supply of nutritional sustainment modules....'"

Makeup: A Key to Good Fish Photos

Don't Forget
the Makeup Kit

"You're going to take your wife where?" Barry Bushrack shouted causing every head in Breadings' Cigar Store to turn in his direction.

"I'm taking her bass fishing tomorrow. She's my favorite fishing partner, and besides, she can fish as well as any man in this joint," I replied.

"What are you, a pinko or something? Women belong in a kitchen, not a boat," he snorted. "A woman's hand was made for brooms and frying pans, not fishing rods."

"I've got news for you, Barry, more than 21 million women now fish in the U.S. and they're pretty good at it," I fired back.

"Don't throw big numbers at me," he retorted. "South Jersey has four million mosquitoes per square foot, so what does that prove?"

"Probably that the folks over there scratch a lot," I answered not fully grasping the weight of his logic.

"Look, John, all you have to do is check the

spelling of the word, and you'll know who is supposed to do the fishing." With that he took a pen from his pocket and scribbled f-i-s-h-e-r-M-E-N on his napkin.

By this time Fred Flatbottom, Sam Waterlog, Bill Backlash, Waldo Hornripple and Hiram Hackwood were convulsed in hysterical laughter. "Hold your ground, Barry," Sam quipped. "There's a lot at stake here."

"I have MY wife under complete control. The ol' battle axe doesn't move without my permission," he bragged. "When I go fishing, it is with the boys or with no one at all."

Barry continued his verbal tirade against women fishing with their husbands, not noticing that his wife, Florescent, had entered through the back door and was standing behind him.

"My wife is o.k. generally, but about the only thing she could catch is a cold," he chuckled. "She's a lot like the coffee in this place—a little weak in the bean!"

"When she comes into a room, the mice jump up on chairs. Her father looked in the crib after she was born and then went down to the zoo and shot the stork."

Nobody at the back table was laughing anymore to say nothing of his wife whose glare nearly melted down the salt shaker.

Curious as to why everybody was staring behind him, Barry spun around only to be met by his wife's fiery stare. Beads of sweat began to form on his brow as he slid down in his chair.

"So I'm weak in the bean, am I?" she barked. "Well, I hope the garage has heat in it because that's where you're going to spend the night! For somebody who has risen from obscurity and is headed toward oblivion, you sure are noisy."

"I can fish you right out of the boat any day and you know it," she added. "Tell the boys about last June's fishing trip when I caught 17 pounds of bass in one morning while you waged a furious battle with one little four-inch bluegill."

All eyes were now on ol' Barry who was dying a slow death. "Tell you what, sport," she asserted. "On the way home you can work on two things. First, a snappy apology and second, a plan for OUR next fishing trip, and it better be a dandy."

Poor Barry! If he just had a more positive outlook on wives fishing with their husbands, he could have saved himself all that grief.

Well, I chose to ignore Bushrack's advice and took my wife, Carolyn, to Carr Lake in Kosciusko County. Carr is a small (79 acres), secluded lake that offers fishermen perfect serenity and some fine bass fishing. There are also sizeable populations of bluegill, crappie and redear sunfish. Best fishing on the lake is in the early spring and late fall after many of the weeds have died off.

It was a windy and chilly April morning, but the sun did make regular appearances to warm things up a bit. We followed all the standard techniques and patterns for this time of the year, but the bass refused to cooperate.

After a brief trip around the north end, I noticed that the wind was churning up the water along the east shore. "That's it!" I shouted. "That's where they're going to be."

We put on Rebel Silver Minnows and began to work the shallow water, and on my second cast a bass smashed the bait with unbridled fury.

As I was fighting the 8-inch monster, my wife said in perfectly calm tones, "I think I might have something."

When I turned around to look, her spinning rod was completely bent over, and the water was churning behind the boat shooting a spray of water three feet into the air.

"You think you've got something," I responded in amazement as I lifted her three and one-half pound bass into the boat. "This is the biggest fish of the day. Nice going."

After seven bass were landed, we headed for shore to call it a day. "You wait here while I get the camera so we can document your catch."

"You can't take my picture this way, I don't have my makeup on," she explained. "What will the people in Warsaw say when they see my picture in *Hoosier Outdoors* Magazine?"

"They'll say, 'Isn't that neat. There's Carolyn—a mother, a college president's wife, a head book-keeper and a down to earth angler! In fact, they will be so intrigued with the two big bass you're holding, they'll probably forget to check for makeup."

"Besides, both those bass are males, and they've spent their whole life around females without makeup on. They won't mind being photographed with you," I concluded.

"Well, o.k., but I know it's going to look just awful."

So the photos were taken, the fish released and another fishing trip was made more memorable by my wife's presence. My dear readers, if you ever see Carolyn, please don't tell her that her face looked like a bleached towel in the photo. MY garage doesn't have any heat in it!

So, all you husbands, why not plan some outings this summer with your best friend and partner. Take along some hot coffee, good lures, a lake map and—oh yes—don't forget the makeup kit!

The Caffeine Jump Start

Coffee, Anyone?

Chills raced up and down my spine, fever flashes reddened my face and my head spun in dizzy disarray as I heard those fateful words early Monday morning.

"We're out of coffee," my wife announced.

A crisis of dramatic proportions had struck my peaceful domicile.

The effective and orderly transition from dreamland to reality is not possible among outdoor types without an early morning infusion of the precious black brew.

"Bluegills will come belly-up laughing when the see me in this bleary-eyed, semi-conscious condition. Real fisherman must begin the day with coffee," I mumbled as I staggered out the back door heading for town and a good ol' fashioned caffeine fix.

Coffee is not only a chemical necessity for the well-adjusted outdoorsman, it is a social necessity that provides an atmosphere within which his and the world's problems can effectively be solved.

If President Clinton really wants to solve the issues surrounding the Los Angeles riots, he should not be talking to congressmen, no matter what the rascals are demanding. That's the crowd, you will remember, that did such a marvelous job on the federal budget, and now they want to solve big city riots?

My advice to the president is to visit any one of Warsaw's morning coffee klatsches where the faithful huddle over steaming bean nectar, and with astonishing leaps of logic, solve hosts of problems before work begins at eight.

In ten minutes flat, for example, the Earl Ellenwood klatsch at John Wong's buried communism in eastern Europe long before Mikhail Gorbachev ever thought of the idea.

Margaret Stutzman and her coffee hounds at Mr. R's Cafe eliminated the federal deficit in a mere five minutes, while Phil Harris' gang at Breadings' solved the even more complex Palestinian controversy in a staggering four minutes and 13 seconds.

It is, I should point out here, a well established fact that a fisherman will tell his most creative lies after a good shot of Juan Valdez's finest. Outdoor types, however, generally agree that decaffeinated coffee is a wimp's beverage—not at all fit for human enjoyment.

Over the years, my keen eyes and impeccable logic have alerted me to the fact that you can actually classify outdoorsman by the way they fix their coffee before a hunting or fishing trip. If a sportsman, for example, drinks the stuff pure black without so much as a glance to check for any floating debris in his cup, you're looking at an ol' fashioned, two-fisted maverick who could survive anywhere.

Cream-with-two-sugars is a person who likes the rugged outdoors, but must modify the sport so as to take some of the bite out of it. You'll probably see this character with a portable TV and CD player on his shoulder as he heads for the wilderness cabin.

Finally, the four-sugars-and-three-creams coffee hound will usually be an outdoor phony. His beverage of choice is a perfect symbol for his aversion to nature. He really likes sweet cream but, so as not to reveal himself as a timid tipple or a wilderness washout, he allows a little coffee to appear in his mug.

Despite the sentiments of a certain popular song, it is not love that makes the world go around, it's coffee. I admit to my passion for the kind of black brew that with a solitary sniff would wake up Rip Van Winkle because I always catch fish after polishing off a couple of cups.

My physician, Dr. Robert Walkabit, keeps mumbling something about the fact that Breadings' coffee will kill me some day.

That may be true, but I feel good about the fact that I will die wide awake.

Of all the beans and seeds on this magnificent planet, I am compelled to rank the coffee bean number one.

This peanut-sized organic unit is the basis of livelihood of more than 25 million people working in 50 different coffee exporting countries. Furthermore, it packs more social and chemical punch than any six other beans combined.

For the record, a cup of coffee can provide the outdoorsman between 75 and 155 milligrams of caffeine, while a similar sized cup of tea contains only 28 to 44 milligrams. That's why tea drinking British sportsmen tend to be more grouchy in the morning than their American counterparts.

Two cups of this powerful black kava and the angler gains a decided edge during his early morning fishing excursions. Bluegills and bass in Winona Lake have no comparable quick fixes. Half asleep when a plastic worm or beetle spin goes cruising past their noses, they are easy prey to the extra alert angler.

You may be amazed by the wide range of caffeine content in a given cup of coffee (75- 155 milligrams). According to Dr. Thorndike Thistlefoot, professor of chemistry at Croaker College, that is due to bean selection, brewing time and cleanness of cups.

The most caffeine-laden cup of coffee in Kosciusko County probably belongs to my friend, Dr. Don Fowler, a specialist in Near Eastern studies, who has not washed his cup in eight years! It has reached a point where he can just add hot water and be sure of at least 175 milligrams of caffeine in his morning brew. Coffee for this sort of sports fan is not a matter of stimulation, but survival itself.

Actually, coffee is the real *tour de force* of every chef in Warsaw. Restaurants rise and fall on the quality of their brew; which immediately causes me to wonder what arcane secret makes Breadings' coffee the unique phenomenon that it is. One cup of Burleigh Burgh's bubbling beverage, and you are a changed person.

Outdoorsmen stagger into that food emporium half awake and within minutes find themselves philosophizing in a manner that would have Aristotle reaching for his dictionary. Estimates are that caffeine concentrations in one cup of that magic mud exceeded 200 milligrams of caffeine prompting the EPA to require Chef Burleigh Burgh to put a catalytic converter on his percolator.

I have probed and prodded, begged and bad-gered Burgh to unveil his formula, but all to no avail. He insists that he will take his secrets with him to the grave. Whatever the secret of his powerful coffee, outdoorsmen love it.

And therein lies the genius of that operation. Give outdoorsmen a cup of battery acid that you can bounce an iron wedge off of, and you'll pack the place out. In the event that you perceive your brew is too weak, just signal Craig Smith. He'll throw one of Burgh's socks into the pot and the brew will immediately take on memorable qualities.

I should hasten to add that, in spite of rumor and reputation, Breadings' does not serve the world's most powerful brew. That honor is reserved for my Arab friend, Ahmad, who can do things to a coffee bean that would shock Juan Valdez and his Columbian cohorts.

In traditional bedouin style, coffee beans are crushed, then boiled for a long period of time result-ing in a thick, bitter, sediment-laden liquid. Served in his tent overlooking the deserts of Jordan, it is without a doubt the best (and most powerful) drink in the world! I love it. It is an outdoorsman's dream come true except that there are no bluegills within thousands of miles to challenge at daybreak.

It should be observed that coffee, among natural commodities in international trade, normally ranks second only to oil in dollar value. It has had a dramatic impact on Japanese society, for example. A generation ago, few Japanese bothered with the brew, but today there are 16,000 coffee houses in Tokyo and more than 100,000 in the nation. You see, being wide awake in the morning does make a difference when you put cars together.

In the light of the coffee bean's strategic value, our government needs to seriously reevaluate its foreign policy. Sure, if Saudi Arabian oil were cut off, all trucks and cars would come to a stop, but should some sadistic Saddam Hussein ever seize control of America's coffee supply lines, the results would be devastating. Morning edginess would never end, and evening doldrums would drain us of our characteristic American spunk.

No longer would the nation know the renewing joy of that idyllic scene: a steaming cup of coffee, an old pot-bellied stove, and good friends in rocking chairs swapping jokes and spinning yarns. That loss would constitute a major blow to the American spirit.

A hint of that special scene can still be found in the breakfast coffee klatsches of Warsaw restaurants where cultural and intellectual horizons are broadened and human spirits lifted. In those havens of the soul the most important question of the morning will be asked by the waitress—"Coffee, anyone?"

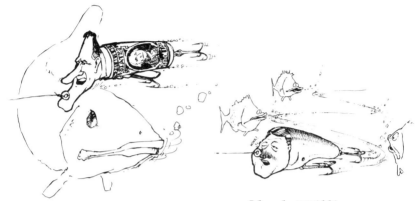

Bushwhacker

**Sleek Willie
Wobbler**

**Quayle
Potatoe Bug**

Perot Popper

Hot New Lures

Tired of getting skunked on Lake Wawasee? Are you frustrated and embarrassed with your lack of success on Winona?

Cheer up. The ol' scribe has been doing solid research this summer, and I have a new fall line-up of lures that will amaze and astound you with their versatility.

Short-sighted fish, murky water, thick vegetation, deep water brush, and high winds that have prevented anglers from catching fish will all be but a vague memory when these lures hit Kosciusko County waters.

Brace yourself, my friends, for an array of lures that is sure to stagger the imagination of even the most skeptical angler.

They are six sure-fire designs specially created for your fall outings on local lakes.

The Bushwhacker - This lure works best over a large, submerged bush where there are lots of hungry fish. Just cast this rubber dollar plug over the starving fish and let it trickle down. Once among the fish, it exhibits a deadly attack strategy.

As the bait is pulled through the water, its lips move and with a gurgling sound it says, "no new hooks, read my lips." While the unsuspecting bass are reading its lips, the lure snags them.

The Saddam Smasher - The idea for this lure originated when I was sitting on the shores of the Tigris River in Iraq. There I observed the value of overwhelming force. You merely flip this lure into a peaceful school of silver bass and it explodes, blasting the surprised fish into the air. Catching dead bass on the way down can be challenging, you know.

The Sleek Willie Wobbler - As most anglers know, the actions of artificial baits are predicable almost to the point of boredom. Not so with the popular, new Sleek Willie Wobbler. Here is a bait that will swerve to the right or left depending on the kind of fish it is approaching. I almost called this lure, "Whiplash Willie," in recognition of what happens to a fish's mental apparatus if it tries to follow this plug.

The Sleek Willie Wobbler can also be bought with an optional "wink mechanism." Many female bass are attracted to it and snap amorously at the lure, while others learn that it has a mate and smash it out of anger. Either way, it hooks them.

Recent polls indicate that 46 percent of the angling public has an interest in this slick moving lure.

All these lures are handmade by the National Organization of Wobblers (NOW) based in Clinton, Arkansas.

The Gore Greenpiece - Here is a lure made just for the non-consumptive environmental angler. This plain, pale green bait is made of soft rubber, has no hooks and lies perfectly still in the water. The general purpose of the lure is to entertain fish, not to catch them.

The Quayle Potatoe Bug - This bait is actually manufactured in England, hence the "e" in potatoe. The lure is remarkable for its ability to work its way through lake sludge and media muck while remaining clean enough to still catch fish.

The Perot Popper - Most artificial baits are designed to stay in the water during the retrieve. Not this one. It pops in and out of the water unpredictably.

This lure catches fish two ways. In Texas, it is cast into the water and reeled in. As it moves past the fish, it organizes them into corporate management units and leads them into large gill nets placed in the water by the angler.

However, since Indiana fish are dramatically smarter than the ones in Texas, the lure operates in a different manner here. You pull it though the water and as it wobbles and gurgles, the bass go belly-up laughing. All the angler has to do is scoop up the giggling fish with a net.

Well, there you have it, gang. Never in the history of lure making has there been such an array of powerful options available to the serious angler.

Should you happen to purchase one of these fall specials and not be satisfied, I cannot guarantee a cash refund, but you will have a choice of: (1) a complimentary lunch with Yassir Arafat at Breadings' Cigar Store or (2) a Dr. Kevorkian Gift Certificate.

War on Bugs

Bomb the Bugs

Like most environmentally sensitive Americans, I wouldn't think of clubbing a seal, shooting a cheetah or skinning an elephant.

A bug crawling up my arm is another matter, however.

You see, I just don't like bugs.

I know the mosquito I just smashed was some mother's little offspring. Somehow, that sentimental relationship just doesn't count when it comes to mosquitoes, ticks or wasps.

My neighbor, Dork Featherstone, gave me a real tongue-lashing last week when he saw me annihilate a mosquito just as it was positioning its apparatus to extract a pint of valuable blood from my leg.

"That little creature might be on the government's endangered specie list. How could you be so thoughtless?" he thundered with pious tones.

Just then another mosquito landed on my leg, and I did the logical thing in response to my neighbor's rebuke. I smiled at the mosquito and punched Dork in the nose.

Don't get me wrong. I am, by nature, a peaceful man.

I like to smell roses, pet cats, feed sparrows, and talk to pigeons.

Bugs, however, were made to be squashed.

I don't like bugs and insects because they have a long history of getting me into trouble.

I was enjoying an outdoor auction at a farm a few years ago, for example, and I merely waved my hand over my head to chase a pesky fly away and almost ended up buying a $356 antique bed pan.

Then there was the time I was awakened at night in my Florida home by the pitter-patter of cockroach feet on our linoleum floor.

I judged the rascal to be the size of a cat so I grabbed a baseball bat that was standing in the corner, tracked the sound down in the dark, and dealt that devil a fatal blow.

When I turned the lights on to view my conquest, I saw the shattered remnants of my wife's new evening shoes lying in a heap at my feet.

Living in a dog house without heat is not fun.

These are not isolated or exotic instances. Just a week ago I had three masterful pages typed on my IBM PS2 for this book when a half-dazed fly landed on the keyboard.

With the greatest of care and skill I rolled up a magazine and clobbered that little wretch with one fatal blow. At that very moment I saw my computer screen go blank. One hour of writing disappeared into thin air.

Flies are thoroughly despicable creatures.

I also detest bugs and insects because they are

smart.

Go to a tropical lake where largemouth bass grow to 15 pounds in three years, and you'll find millions of bugs. Bugs aren't stupid. They like tropical paradises, too.

Flies, gnats, ants and spiders always sit immediately outside your kitchen door. Just open it once on a summer night, and these miserable creatures will make themselves at home.

Let me assure all you armchair psychiatrists that I am not paranoic or irrational in my response to bugs.

Remember, I like caterpillars and nightcrawlers. Wiggly friends like these I can abide, but bugs and insects must go. You can't put bugs on a decent sized fish hook, they buzz in your ears and they make lousy pets.

I don't care if the Fort Wayne Friends of Animals Society pickets my house for a year; when a bug lands on my nose, he's going to get massacred.

Scientists tell me that for every American there are no less than 41,000 mosquitoes. Just think of how much time you're going to spend slapping yourself this summer.

The female mosquito will bite one to four times during her seasonal life span, her targets including birds and animals as well as humans.

World Health Organization statistics indicate that one person dies somewhere every 30 seconds as the result of a mosquito bite.

Catch this item, men. Only female mosquitoes attack in order to nourish their eggs with your blood. The males are vegetarians. Females can normally lay 100-300 eggs after each blood meal.

Worldwide, there are 2,500 different species of

mosquitoes (more than 150 in the United States) which spread 80 different diseases including malaria and yellow fever.

These are the wretched creatures Dork Featherstone wanted to protect for future generations!

Already my closets, patio, bedroom, office, and boat have stacks of Raid, bug repellent, and giant swatters. Summer means war.

Save the eagles, whales and otters, but bomb the bugs!

Best Therapy

Surgery and Sunfish

All things considered, prostate surgery in the middle of the fishing season is not my all-time favorite activity.

It was about a year ago that I was informed by my long-time and very competent family physician, Dr. Walkabit, that I had an enlarged prostate. In case you don't recognize the name, he's the one who gained international fame last year by performing the world's first hernia transplant.

He is also responsible for inventing the 10 1/2 month pregnancy test for women. It's a little slower than other tests, but it's deadly accurate. The Walkabit Pacemaker with a dimmer switch is a hit in retirement centers across America.

Dr. Walkabit counselled that I would probably need surgery in the near future, so I was directed to Dr. Gordie Goodflat, who is regarded as one of the finest urologists in the state of Indiana.

A man's choice of doctor is second only in importance to his choice of wife. I can confirm this from a rather pointed lesson I learned in London a few years ago.

Needing a shot for a nasty sore throat and fever, I came upon a Dr. Anthony Wilson, MA, MB, B.Chir. (Cham.), MRCS (Eng.), LRCP (London), LSA. I figured that anyone with that education and certification from the Royal College of Physicians and Surgeons had to be top-notch.

I should have been alert to the fact something was amiss, however, on discovering his waiting room was empty, the reading material was dull to the point of narcosis and the ceiling lamp was half-filled with dead flies.

The penicillin delivered to my posterior with a one foot, thoroughly dull needle makes me cringe every time I hear the word London. He must have gotten that syringe out of a WW I medical field kit. My finger prints can still be seen on the ceiling of his office.

In contrast to the above nightmare, the choice of Dr. Goodflat for the surgical procedure was perfect. His intense and genuine concern for his patients was more than evident and the surgery (transurethral resection) was performed with consummate skill.

There was only one flaw in Dr. Goodflat's handling of this whole matter, and it was his insistence that after surgery I could not go fishing in a boat. "No climbing stairs, extensive rides in cars, lifting heavy objects or fishing in a boat" were his exact words.

Now I ask you, how could such a brilliant surgeon not recognize the very effective therapy fishing from a boat could provide? I went to six other doctors for additional opinions and all agreed, "no fishing from a boat."

It is my judgment that what we're dealing with here is a very subtle medical conspiracy. What is it with doctors and their aversion to water?

After some heavy pondering, I realized why virtually all physicians suffer from subliminal aquaphobia. They all play golf, and the one thing they fear most is having their $7.95 Ben Hogan golf ball drop into a water hazard.

When I arrived at Kosciusko Community Hospital, I checked in and was given a gown that was cut on the half shell and held shut in the back by two unreachable strings.

That fashion piece made me look like a cross between a cook and an undertaker's assistant. "Who designed these crazy things and what did they hope to accomplish?" I asked myself.

The answer came when I attempted to walk briskly up the hallway in that thing only to have the accompanying wind lift it straight up in all directions bringing applause from three rooms. It is clearly intended to deter recovering male patients from pursuing nurses.

I was prepared for a 7:30 a.m. surgery at 6:00 a.m. and greeted warmly by the very competent anesthesiologist, Dr. Solomon Snooze. He suggested a local anesthetic, but I insisted on something imported. To my sheer amazement he put me to sleep faster than a Lloyd Benson treasury speech.

When I finally returned from Snooze's wonderland, I found myself in room 415 where I was later joined by Filbert Fern. The nurses were absolutely superb in their professionalism and efficiency. I mean, it really takes a special dedication to carry out gallons of bloody urine and come back smiling at the patient!

The next few days were full of ills, pills and chills. Fern had hordes of people bursting through the door wanting to see him and hear all the details of his injury. I even suggested that the nurses set up a grand stand to accommodate what looked like the entire Church of God population of Indiana.

One small chair more than adequately accommodated the occasional visitor who came to see the ol' scribe. Of course, Fern had the advantage of a really neat injury. He had broken his ankle in three places and had two screws put in the bones. People eagerly wanted to see the ankle and hear his tale of woe.

Now tell me, friends, who is going to drive 25 miles to talk about my prostate gland? Filbert had a perfect show-and-tell operation, but what exactly could I show and tell about? Dr. Goodflat had a suggestion which I nixed forthrightly.

Finally, I was released from the hospital and proceeded to develop pleurisy and pneumonia which made for some very exciting (and painful) days. Emergency room doctors did a good job of diagnosis and prescription, but the ultimate explanation for my good recovery was bluegill fishing from my pier on Chapman Lake.

The physical and psychological benefits from panfishing are remarkable and deserve proper notice in the *Journal of the American Medical Society*.

When the first chunky bluegill ripped the bobber from the glassy surface of the water and proceeded to arrogantly battle the ol' scribe on ultra-light equipment, the pain disappeared.

I guess I had forgotten the eloquent, yet simple joys of bank fishing for bluegills. Four-pound test line, an ultra-light rod with an open faced spinning reel, a slip bobber, two split shot, a small hook and a juicy night crawler (personally blessed by Rev. Farnsworth) made for a perfect evening.

The preponderant medical opinion kept me from fishing from a boat, but the view from my lounge chair on the pier was just as impressive.

That serene, relaxed encounter with sunsets and sunfish was but a gentle reminder of the greatness of God—creator of life and healer of body.

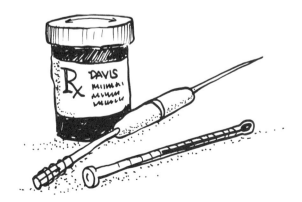

The Camp Cook

Keep an Eye
on the Cook

The best advice I ever received from my ol' hunting buddy, Stu Steelshot, was "never take your eye off the camp cook."

As a 16-year-old hunting enthusiast living in South Jersey, I never really thought much about the dangers of hunting in the Pine Barrens or anywhere, for that matter, until he described for me the disasters that can be created by a cook.

Later, at a fishing lodge in Wisconsin, I came to understand what Stu had in mind. A brawny, unshaven cook served us a soup that had an ominous green hue to it, and by the next morning the entire camp was beating a path to the outhouses with what is commonly known as Baghdad Belly (or, more affectionately, "The Mexican Quick Step").

"Never let the camp cook out of your sight during meal times," Stu advised me on more than one occasion.

"If he passes up the barbecued possum ribs, you

know they probably fell on the floor in the kitchen, or he discovered mice nibbling on them prior to serving time."

I don't want to cast unjustified aspersions on these dedicated practitioners of the culinary arts, but I feel some obligation as an outdoor writer to help innocent sportsmen survive their first outing.

Experience and a lot of Alka Seltzer tell me that greasy-pawed, spatula-wielding cooks are a greater threat to fishing and hunting fraternities than all the anti-hunting lobbies, polluters, pseudo-ecologists and politicians put together.

During a recent lapse of sanity, I visited Mike Mildew, a crusty ol' camp cook, at his run-down cabin in Michigan. I made it a point to visit him at 3:00 in the afternoon so he would not feel any obligation to feed me. My insurance does not cover voluntary food poisoning.

That visit, gang, was a near fatal mistake!

"Good to see you, John," he said through a mostly toothless smile. "I haven't seen you for ten years. How are things in ol' Warsaw, anyhow?

"The town is growing fast, but the fishing on our three lakes is still great." I responded.

"Well, that's good to hear. Say, you're just in time to sample my newest creation, 'Sizzling Muskrat Steaks.'"

You just don't say "no" to ol' Mike when he offers you one of his dishes, unless, of course, you have a passionate desire for substantial amounts of verbal abuse.

I could just envision my stomach raising a white surrender flag as the dark brown chunks of meat dripping with possum grease slid down my gullet.

Dessert consisted of pickled creek mussels with

whipped cream.

I'm glad to report that I survived the ordeal avoiding Montezuma's Revenge, but not without generous help from Rolaids, Alka-Seltzer and Pepto-Bismol.

The main dish the next night was not much better. I was cutting into what was announced as "Gourmet Groundhog," when I hit a flea collar.

Most camp or lodge cooks do attempt to make meals interesting and attractive. Harvey Fern, senior chef at Foggy Hollow Fishing Lodge, served deer meat one day and asked the kids to guess what it was, saying, "I'll give you a hint: It's what your mother sometimes calls your father."

"Don't anybody eat that meat," a little boy shouted. "It's jackass."

Camp breakfasts usually consist of burned toast, scrambled eggs with shell fragments and blackened bacon —a lot like the Breadings' Cigar Store early morning "Blue Plate Special."

The real *tour de force* of the camp chef, however, is that morning cup of black mud, known affectionately by some locals as embalming fluid.

While such battery acid helps make the transition from dreamland to reality pass quickly, it also does disastrous things to the plumbing systems of the most hearty of outdoorsmen.

Sam Waterlog, owner and chief cook at a run-down joint in South Jersey, used to make a cup of coffee so strong that you could bounce an iron wedge off it. "It's got to have body to it or it's not worth the price," he used to say to customers as they staggered out the door."

For some reason, cooks regard measuring spoons as an unnecessary annoyance and, as a result, one pot may be so weak it hardly has color, while another would hold a large spoon upright indefinitely.

Such challenges to the human digestive system have not diminished the affection American sportsmen and women have for the black brew, however. Its jolting effect to the otherwise slumbering and lethargic body is most welcomed when the outdoorsmen can only fish from 4:30 a.m. to 7:00 a.m. Drinking coffee in public also provides the opportunity for numerous pranks.

My friend, Arnie Adenoid, for example, whose intellectual abilities peaked at age five, once thought it would be great sport to spice my cup of coffee with generous amounts of cayenne pepper.

Seconds after I took one sip of that enriched brew I swung into wild movements that break-dancers haven't even thought of yet.

Occasionally, the most memorable thing about coffee is not the taste, but the manner in which it is served. Breadings' Burleigh Burgh, winner of the 1992 golden stomach pump award, for example, will simply dazzle you with his agility and coordination when pouring a cup of coffee.

That rascal can pour his lumpy brew without spilling a drop, gather up dirty dishes and holler at half a dozen customers all at the same time!

Oh yes, some sage advice for outdoorsmen who want to avoid getting clobbered by the camp cook: never suggest he wear a hair net!

Willie's "Necessary" Equipment

Critical Equipment

Willie Woodslab was in deep trouble.

He had received his new fishing catalog from Bass Pro Shops just when his cabin fever was at its worst. In an advanced state of piscatorial delirium, he purchased $1,413.27 worth of new gadgets for the $19,500 bass boat he had bought last year.

I was enjoying some of Willie's black brew at the breakfast table when his wife, Gardenia, came thundering though the door with a crumpled MasterCard receipt in her hand.

"This is the living end," she protested while positioning her well-rounded, 250-pound frame at the end of the table. "You dropped us below the poverty line when you bought that stupid bass boat. Now you've got the gall to buy more junk for that floating tackle shop."

"As I explained last year, it's a matter of economics," Willie thundered back confidently. "Being out on Lake Wawasee without a 150-horse motor, a Z-6000 Liquid Crystal Graph fish finder, a pH meter, a Color-C-Lector, a temperature gauge, and a gallon of Fish Formula II makes no sense at all. I could spend valuable hours fishing and catch nothing, thus losing money."

"These slick new electronic instruments will improve my bass catching ability by more than 50 percent, which means more fish on the table and less time and money spent at the store. Just think of the savings in our budget."

"Savings! Of course, why didn't I think of that?" she replied with cutting sarcasm. "Now let's see. You went on a fishing trip to Florida last year that cost $1,185, took the $19,500 boat and $813 worth of tackle with you for a grand investment of $21,498."

"Then, as I recall, you returned home with a total of nine pounds of fish fillets. If my calculations are correct, that fish cost us $2,388.66 a pound. Why the savings were enormous," she replied caustically.

Now, friends, most outdoor types of the male gender would have retreated and retrenched for a later assault. Not Willie, however. With reckless abandon he carried on.

"Look, Gardenia, I didn't complain when you spent $1.50 for a pair of shoes at the Nearly New Shop. I even helped you buy a new frying pan and broom out of last week's paycheck."

Now Gardenia was furious.

"Look, sport, one more outburst of your patronizing generosity and these knuckles are gonna rearrange your facial anatomy."

Clenching a fist that must have measured a good 10-inches in circumference, she produced a very powerful argument.

Searching for a defense that would allow him to save face, Willie shouted triumphantly, "You can lead a horse to water, but you can't make him surf." (Willie never was good at old sayings).

"Furthermore, I discussed the equipment with Burleigh Burgh at Breadings' Cigar Store, and he thought it was a good idea," he added.

"Oh, yeah, I remember Burgh," Gardenia responded thoughtfully. "He's the guy who thinks a garlic press is an Italian newspaper. Didn't he talk you into investing in his Teflon-coated peanut butter that was not supposed to stick to the roof of your mouth?"

"Then, there was the new restaurant chain he wanted you to support featuring rabbit burgers. He was going to call it 'Bunny King—Home of the Hopper.' That little adventure cost us a mere $5,000."

"Let's not forget Burgh's chocolate-covered lobsters or the electric tuba he invented for high school marching bands. These dandies added up to a cool $1,450," she shouted defiantly.

"For a mere $295 you were able to purchase 50-pounds of powdered water from Burgh, but you never did find anything you could add to it. Yeah, Willie, you really latched onto an economic giant when you took advice from Burleigh Burgh."

Stunned by this potent analysis and its irrefutable implications, Willie just sat there with a coffee-stained napkin in his hand and stared into space.

Finally, he looked into Gardenia's bloodshot eyes and humbly announced, "Honey, you're right. I spent too much money on bass fishing equipment. I think I'll sell all of it and buy much cheaper fly fishing equipment I can use for bluegills. Using flies as fishing lures is really economical."

"Well, that's okay if you want to," Gardenia responded sweetly, "but I don't know why any bluegill would be dumb enough to bite a zipper."

Gardenia is strong on economics, but not too good on fishing lures.